Sienna Strawberry and the ice palace ballet

Published by Top That! Publishing plc
Tide Mill Way, Woodbridge, Suffolk, IP12 1AP, UK
www.topthatpublishing.com
Copyright © 2011 Top That! Publishing plc
All rights reserved
0 2 4 6 8 9 7 5 3 1
Printed and bound in China

D1133787

What scene have the
children made today?

A land of ice and snow...

One day, Sienna Strawberry stepped into the children's playscene. The children had created a land of ice and snow.

Sienna had always wanted to be a famous ballerina.

She loves spinning and twirling in her favorite tutu and ballet shoes.

Sienna looked around the icy land and saw Apps Apple and Tessa Tomato playing in the snow.

"There you are, Sienna," said Tessa. "We've got some exciting news!"

"There is an ice palace beyond the frozen rivers and lakes," said Apps. "Every year, the princess holds a special dance there."

"You should audition, Sienna," said Tessa.

Sienna was very excited!

"But what if I forget the steps at my audition?" asked Sienna, suddenly feeling very nervous.

"Don't worry, Sienna," said Apps. "You are a brilliant dancer. You just need to practice."

So, Sienna set off towards the ice palace.

Finally, Sienna arrived at the ice palace and saw an amazing stage, set for a ballet performance.

Sienna looked at the other ballerinas practicing on the stage and started to feel very nervous again. She turned around and saw one of the ballerinas smiling at her.

"**H**ave you come to audition?" asked the ballerina.

"Yes, but I'm a bit nervous," admitted Sienna.

Sienna began to dance and, although she missed a few steps, the ballerina thought she was very good.

"I think we have the perfect role for you!" smiled the ballerina.

Sienna began to practice, but she could
not remember all the routine.

The ballerinas tried to help Sienna,
but no matter what they did,
Sienna kept forgetting her steps.

Feeling very upset, Sienna began to cry.

"Sienna, what's wrong?" cried Apps and Tessa, who had followed Sienna to the ice palace.

"I can't remember any of the steps in my dance!" sobbed Sienna.

"Don't worry, Sienna," said Tessa.

"You just need to practice!" said Apps.

So, Sienna went to find a quiet spot to practice her routine.

Sienna practiced and practiced until finally, she could remember all the steps to her routine and danced her part beautifully.

Sienna was on her way back to the stage when she saw the princess crying.

"What's wrong?" asked Sienna.

"I'm supposed to be leading the ice dance tonight," sobbed the beautiful princess. "But I've hurt my ankle. If only someone could take my place," she cried.

Sienna had been practicing her routine all day and she felt very confident about remembering her steps.

"If you like," said Sienna. "I could dance in your place. I have been practicing all day."

"That would be wonderful!" said the princess.

So, Sienna went back to the stage. When she arrived the other ballerinas told her that, because she was dancing the princess's part, she must learn a new routine!

Suddenly, Sienna felt very nervous again.

But, she knew what she needed to do.

Finally, it was time for the ice dance to begin. Sienna waited nervously by the edge of the stage.

Then, the music started and it was time for Sienna's big moment.

Sienna stepped out onto the stage and began to dance.

And once she started, she just listened to the music and danced with all her heart.

Sienna danced brilliantly and remembered all her steps.

"You were brilliant, Sienna!" said the princess. "Well done!"

Sienna had always wanted to be a famous ballerina and now, in the land of ice and snow, she was.

Sienna no longer worries about forgetting her dance routines because now she knows that to be a famous ballerina, practice makes perfect!